Helena

Bert

Katherine

PEX PIG

Piggy

Elephant

What do these animals do when they are home alone?

For Bibi, Fluffy, Spots, Tiger, Porky, Rabbit, Wrinkles, Helena, 5307,
Turbo, and the hamster whose name I forgot (Sorry!).

© 2009 Copyright text and illustrations by Loes Riphagen
First published in the Netherlands under the title *Huisbeestenboel*
© Uitgeverij De Fontein, 2009.
Graphic Design: Zeno
All rights reserved.

ISBN 978-1-934734-55-1

Published by Seven Footer Kids, an imprint of Seven Footer Press,
a division of Seven Footer Entertainment, LLC, New York

© 2011 Copyright Seven Footer Kids for US and Canada English edition
All Rights Reserved

Manufactured in Shen Zhen, Guang Dong, P.R. China, in 12/10 by Printplus Limited.
10 9 8 7 6 5 4 3 2

LOES RIPHAGEN

Animals Home Alone

Seven Footer Kids

REWARD!

What is on Petey's beak?

Why was Charles angry?

What was Bibi looking for?

How did Arnold, Sylvester, and Bruce end up in the sewer?

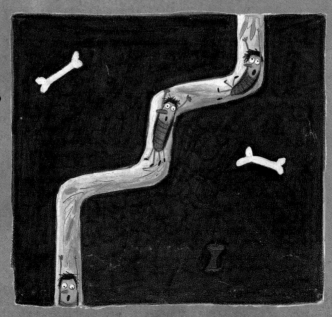

Can you find Buzz, Flap, Flit, and Chew on every page?